W9-CNH-373

Dad's
Van

Crabtree Publishing Company
www.crabtreebooks.com
1-800-387-7650

PMB 16A, 350 Fifth Ave.
Suite 3308,
New York, NY

616 Welland Ave.
St. Catharines, ON
L2M 5V6

Published by Crabtree Publishing in 2010

Series Editor: Jackie Hamley
Editors: Melanie Palmer, Reagan Miller
Series Advisor: Dr. Hilary Minns
Series Designer: Peter Scoulding
Editorial Director: Kathy Middleton

Text © Mick Gowar 2008
Illustration © Rory Walker 2008

The rights of the author and the illustrator
of this Work have been asserted.

The author and publisher
would like to thank Robert
Kearney for permission to use
the photograph on page 4 (top)

First published in 2008
by Franklin Watts
(A division of Hachette
Children's Books)

**Library and Archives Canada
Cataloguing in Publication**

Gowar, Mick, 1951-
    Dad's van / Mick Gowar ; illustrated by
Rory Walker.

(Tadpoles)
ISBN 978-0-7787-3866-4 (bound).--
ISBN 978-0-7787-3897-8 (pbk.)

    1. Readers (Primary). 2. Readers--
Family vacations. I. Walker, Rory II. Title.
III. Series: Tadpoles (St. Catharines, Ont.)

PE1117.T33 2009a   428.6   C2009-903984-2

**Library of
Congress
Cataloging-in-Publication Data**

Gowar, Mick, 1951-
 Dad's van / by Mick Gowar ; illustrated by
Rory Walker.
     p. cm. -- (Tadpoles)
 Summary: When Dad's van will not start while
the family is on vacation, Mom suggests a
surprising solution to the problem.
 ISBN 978-0-7787-3897-8 (pbk. : alk. paper) -- ISBN
978-0-7787-3866-4 (reinforced lib. bdg. : alk. paper)
[1. Vans--Fiction. 2. Family life--Fiction.
3. Vacations--Fiction. 4. Humorous stories.]
I. Walker, Rory, ill. II. Title. III. Series.

PZ7.G747Dd 2009
[E]--dc22
                                                    2009025292

Dad's Van

by Mick Gowar

Illustrated by Rory Walker

Crabtree Publishing Company

www.crabtreebooks.com

Mick Gowar

"I like the way all of the family try to help Dad with the van. Does it remind you of any other stories about helping people?"

Rory Walker

"This story reminds me of my dad's old, custard-colored car. It had big white wings too, but it didn't break down as often as this van!"

It was holiday time.

But the van would
not start.

"I will have to push," said Dad.

"I will help," said Mom.

"We will help," said
Emma and Sam.

"Woof!" said Alfie.
"Meow!" said Dina.

"Squawk!" said Pedro.
"Squeak!" said Peanut.

"The van is started!"
said Dad.

14

15

"Who is driving?"
asked Mom.
"Not me," said Dad.

"Not us," said
Emma and Sam.

"STOP!"

everybody cried.

19

The van stopped ...
and would not go.

"We will have to push," said Dad.

21

But Mom said, "No,
I have a better idea!"

Notes for adults

TADPOLES are structured to provide support for early readers. The stories may also be used by adults for sharing with young children.

Starting to read alone can be daunting. **TADPOLES** help by providing visual support and repeating high frequency words and phrases. These boo[ ] will both develop confidence and encourage reading and rereading for pleasure.

If you are reading this book with a child, here are a few suggestions

1. Make reading fun! Choose a time to read when you and the child are relaxed and have time to share the story.
2. Talk about the story before you start reading. Look at the cover and the blurb. What might the story be about? Why might the child like it?
3. Encourage the child to reread the story, and to retell the story in their own words, using the illustrations to remind them what has happened.
4. Discuss the story and see if the child can relate it to their own experiences, or perhaps compare it to another story they know.
5. Give praise! Children learn best in a positive environment.

If you enjoyed this book, why not try another TADPOLES story?

At the End of the Garden
9780778738503 RLB
9780778738817 PB

Bad Luck, Lucy!
9780778738510 RLB
9780778738824 PB

Ben and the Big Balloon
9780778738602 RLB
9780778738916 PB

Crabby Gabby
9780778738527 RLB
9780778738831 PB

Dad's Cake
9780778738657 RLB
9780778738961 PB

Dad's Van
9780778738664 RLB
9780778738978 PB

The Dinosaur Next Door
9780778738732 RLB
9780778739043 PB

Five Teddy Bears
9780778738534 RLB
9780778738848 PB

I'm Taller Than You!
9780778738541 RLB
9780778738855 PB

Leo's New Pet
9780778738558 RLB
9780778738862 PB

Little Troll
9780778738565 RLB
9780778738879 PB

Mop Top
9780778738572 RLB
9780778738886 PB

My Auntie Susan
9780778738589 RLB
9780778738893 PB

My Big, New Bed
9780778738596 RLB
9780778738909 PB

Night, Night
9780778738671 RLB
9780778738985 PB

Over the Moon!
9780778738688 RLB
9780778738992 PB

Pirate Pete
9780778738619 RLB
9780778738923 PB

Rooster's Alarm
9780778738749 RLB
9780778739050 PB

Runny Honey
9780778738626 RLB
9780778738930 PB

The Sad Princess
9780778738725 RLB
9780778739036 PB

Sammy's Secret
9780778738633 RLB
9780778738947 PB

Sam's Sunflower
9780778738640 RLB
9780778738954 PB

Tag!
9780778738695 RLB
9780778739005 PB

Ted's Party Bus
9780778738701 RLB
9780778739012 PB

Tortoise Races Home
9780778738718 RLB
9780778739029 PB